The Journey of Teddy and Technology Star

Xiaoli Huan and Ron Shehane

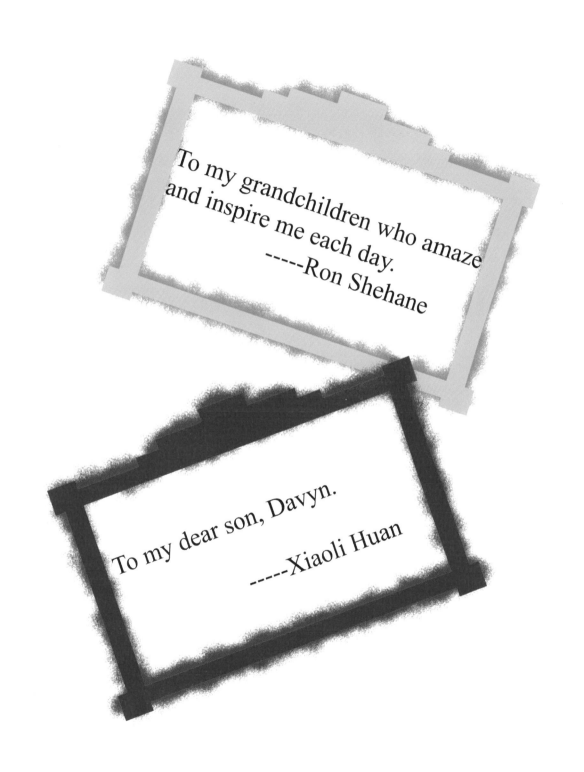

To my grandchildren who amaze and inspire me each day.

-----Ron Shehane

To my dear son, Davyn.

-----Xiaoli Huan

Teddy, Puppy and Lion are best buddies. They go to school together. They like to play soccer, especially Teddy. Teddy thinks he can run faster than Lion and Puppy.

Teddy, Puppy and Lion also like to drop by the ice cream shop in the neighborhood. The ice cream shop makes yummy ice cream. The three best friends share stories while eating. They talk, laugh and have a lot of fun.

One day, Teddy got a video game for his birthday. "Wow cool," Teddy gasped, "Now I can play it every day." "But my father says we should only play video games on weekends and it should be after we finish all school work," Lion told Teddy.

"Video games are fun. I hope to play them all day. I heard these cool games are made from smart technologies." Teddy said. That night, Teddy played video games long after bedtime. There was a shining star outside Teddy's window that he had not seen before. The star stayed with Teddy all night long while he played the video game.

Teddy got up so late that he missed his favorite classes.
He also felt sleepy all day.

Teddy took the video game everywhere he would go. "Teddy, can you play with us," Puppy asked. "You are still my best friend," said Teddy, "even when I can't play with you, right?" "Yea... but you are never here," sighed Lion, "Don't you think friends should spend time together, talk, share and laugh? A friend shows how much he cares." "The video game is such fun. I just cannot stop it," said Teddy.

Teddy kept playing games all day and night. Still that shining star outside Teddy's window stayed with Teddy all night long.

One day, in Teddy's favorite PE class, there was a soccer ball game. Teddy kept his feet moving while trying to focus his eyes on the soccer ball. He felt the soccer field blurring. It was hard for him to see just like on a foggy day. His head began to spin and his face turned red and sweaty. "What is happening to me?"

The coach thought Teddy needed a rest.
Teddy felt sad as he sat on a bench alone.

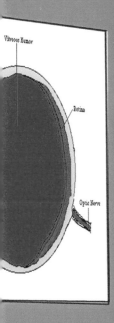

Teddy's parents said, "Oh my, we need to see the doctor about Teddy's eyes. Teddy, you may need to wear glasses. Is this the reason you got bad grades on the math test?" Teddy's parents worried.

That night, Teddy could not sleep. He was trying to figure out what was wrong. Teddy thought, "Since I got the video game, I got bad grades in school, lost my friends, and now have problems with my eyes... Aren't video games supposed to make people happier, but why am I not happy now?" Teddy asked himself. As Teddy lay in his bed, he saw a shining star falling from the sky into his room. The star was crying.

Teddy asked: "You look familiar. Why are you so sad?" The star said: "I am a technology star made for children to discover and learn knowledge. I am smart and funny. I am supposed to shine in the sky, but tonight I fell." "Oh, what can I do to help you to return to the sky?" Teddy felt sorry for the star. "There is a way to lead me to the sky, but there are three doors on the way. The doors are locked and can only be opened by solving puzzles that are in front of each door." "Do not worry. I will help you." Teddy comforted Star.

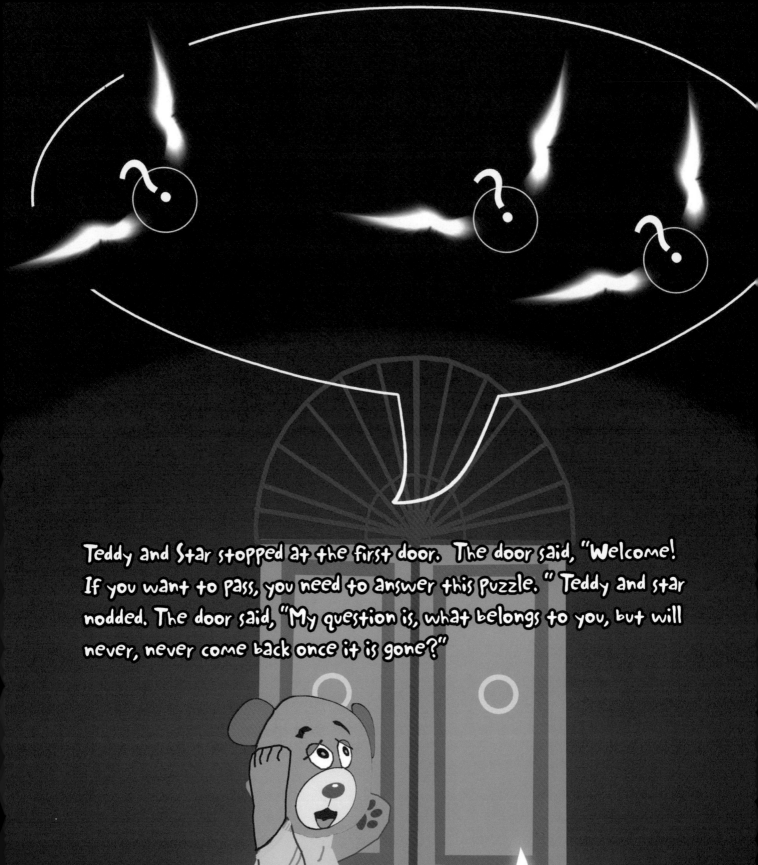

Teddy and Star stopped at the first door. The door said, "Welcome! If you want to pass, you need to answer this puzzle." Teddy and star nodded. The door said, "My question is, what belongs to you, but will never, never come back once it is gone?"

Teddy said, "What is that? Not a toy, because I still can buy a new one if a toy is lost. Money? No, I can earn more allowance if I help my parents on chores." Teddy started to think really hard. He thought of the time he had wasted that would never come back. It was those days when he played video games. "Yes! It is the time! It belonged to me, but once it passed, it never comes back!"

"You are right!" The door was happy about the answer and let Teddy and Star in. Teddy and Star were able to climb to the second door.

"You won't get it so easily this time!" The second door said seriously. "My question is which object does not belong to this group. The group has: TV, computer, video game, flower, and toy car."

"The flower is alive and seems different from others in the group," Teddy thought, "The others do not have any life. However, they can help people when they are used correctly and for good." So Teddy decided to choose "flower" as the answer.

"You are a smart boy!" The second door accepted the answer, "Remember all technologies such as TVs, computers, and video games are just tools and they should be used correctly so they can help people. You are the master of technologies. Do not let them steal your precious time!" The second door then opened for Teddy and little Star.

Teddy and little Star continued their journey. They saw a clown in front of the third door that was trying to balance himself on a ball while holding big blocks in each hand. The clown kept falling off the ball. "Do you need help?" Teddy asked. "Yes, I think so. I am trying to balance myself, but it is hard," the clown said. "You seem to have too much weight on the left side," Teddy said. "Can you help me? If you do, I will give you the key to the third door," the clown said.

Teddy started to think, "There are 5 blocks that were labeled 'work' on the right side and 7 blocks on the left side that were labeled 'free and fun'. 7-5 = 2. Yes, I need to take away two blocks from the left side, so the clown can balance himself." Once Teddy helped the clown to take away the extra "free and fun" blocks, the clown was perfectly balanced. Teddy thought, "I love doing nothing but fun things, but that is too much. I should balance fun and work." "Thank you for the help!" The clown happily opened the third door for Teddy and little Star.

Teddy and Star were successfully through all three doors. Teddy hung the star in the sky with all the other stars. "Thank you for helping me, Teddy," the little star said. "Please remember to balance your time with all technologies, so you can keep me in the sky." "I surely will, Star," Teddy answered.

From then on, Teddy only played his video game a little on Saturdays. This gave him lots of time to talk, laugh and have fun with Lion and Puppy. Teddy was also doing great in school and felt really happy because his heart was full.

Quizzes

a) We only do things that are fun.   True or False

b) The more you play video games,
the happier you will be.   True or False

c) The more you watch TV,
the smarter you will be.   True or False

d) A friend is someone who is there for you.   True or False

e) We can do whatever we want to
do without following our parents' rules.   True or False

f) If we use technologies in a correct and balanced
way, they can make our life a lot easier.   True or False

g) It is good for your health to play video games
or watch TV while you eat.   True or False

h) If a time passes, it will come back again.   True or False

i) We can balance our work
with free and fun time.   True or False

j) Sports and exercises are good for your health.   True or False

LaVergne, TN USA
02 December 2010
206953LV00005B